ONE WINTER'S NIGHT

ONE WINTER'S
~ NIGHT ~

Primrose Lockwood
Illustrations by Elaine Mills

Macmillan Publishing Company
New York

Maxwell Macmillan International Publishing Group
New York   Oxford   Singapore   Sydney

Macmillan Publishing Company is part of the
Maxwell Communication Group of Companies.

Macmillan Publishing Company
866 Third Avenue
New York, NY 10022
First published by Heinemann Young Books, London, England.
First American edition
Printed in Hong Kong.

10 9 8 7 6 5 4 3 2 1

Library of Congress Cataloging-in-Publication Data
Lockwood, Primrose.
One winter's night / by Primrose Lockwood ; illustrations by Elaine Mills. — 1st American ed.
            p.   cm
"First published by Heinemann Young Books, London, England"—T.p. verso.
Summary: Joseph's wish is fulfilled when his father brings him a puppy.
ISBN 0-02-759235-9
[1. Dogs—Fiction.] I. Mills, Elaine, ill. II. Title.
PZ7.L8190n 1991   [E]—dc20   90-22891

For my nephew Joseph and his dog Timmy
and for Ben, Oliver, Lucy and Laura Sophie
at the farm on the hill.
P.L.

For Jenny
E.M.

Over a house the moon is shining.
Next to the house some trees are growing.
Inside the house a fire is burning.
Beside the fire a boy is sitting.
His name is Joseph.
What is he thinking?

From out of the house a man is going.
He's wearing a coat for the wind is blowing.
He's climbing the hill, but where is he going?
Where is he going now the moon is shining?
He's Joseph's father.
An owl is calling.

At the top of the hill there's a farmhouse standing.
It's silver and gray for the moon is shining.
Towards the farmhouse Joseph's father is striding.
From out of the shadows a fox is slinking.
It's frosty and cold.
The fox is watching.

In front of the farmhouse a gate is creaking.
Joseph's father goes through it. The gate he's latching.
The path to the house is long and winding.
In a barn somewhere a dog is barking.
Joseph's father goes up to the farmhouse door.
Why has he come? What is he seeking?

Inside the farmhouse children are listening.
Around a big table they're busily working.
One of them shouts, "Joseph's father is knocking!"
Along the passage their parents are hurrying.
They open the door.
Joseph's father is waiting.

With the moon to guide them the yard they're crossing.
From the window the children are watching.
They are leaning out and excitedly waving.
Across the yard the barn door is banging.
It's dark in the barn,
But a lamp is glowing.

Inside the barn the friends are talking.
Joseph's father is carefully looking.
When he comes out, a box he's carrying.
Inside the box something is moving.
He's taking the box to the house down the hill.
"Take care! Take care!" the children are calling.

At the house on the hill time is passing.
The hour is late. Joseph is sleeping.
His mother is busy. What is she making?
Down the hillside his father is coming.
Safe in his hands
Is the box he's carrying.

Early next morning Joseph is waking.
Into his room his parents are going.
They carry a box. "Come and see," they're calling.

Into the box Joseph is looking.
A puppy is there.
His tail is wagging.

"The puppy is yours," his parents are saying.
"Mine!" Joseph cries, hardly believing.
Carefully, carefully, the puppy he's holding.
Secretly, gently, its soft head he's stroking.
The puppy feels safe.
Joseph is smiling.

Out in the garden Joseph is running.
The puppy's there too, excitedly barking.
Laughing and leaping,
Together they're playing.

On the house on the hill,
The first flakes are falling.